DREAMCATCHER

by AUDREY OSOFSKY

illustrated by ED YOUNG

Orchard Books   New York

JE

I WISH TO THANK the Minnesota Historical Society and the pioneer work of Frances Densmore.
As a child she "heard an Indian drum," and followed its call until she was ninety, visiting
Ojibway villages to record their songs on wax cylinders and study their culture. In her books
I heard the call of the Indian drum. — A.O.

Text copyright © 1992 by Audrey Osofsky. Illustrations copyright © 1992 by Ed Young.

Orchard Books, 95 Madison Avenue, New York, NY 10016

Manufactured in the United States of America. Printed by General Offset Company, Inc.
Bound by Horowitz/Rae. Book design by Mina Greenstein
The text of this book is set in 16 point Usherwood Medium. The illustrations are pastel reproduced in full color.
10   9   8   7

Library of Congress Cataloging-in-Publication Data
Osofsky, Audrey. Dreamcatcher / by Audrey Osofsky ; illustrated by Ed Young.   p.   cm.   Summary: In the land of
the Ojibway a baby sleeps, protected from bad dreams, as the life of the tribe goes on around him.
ISBN 0-531-05988-X.   ISBN 0-531-08588-0 (lib. bdg.)
[1. Ojibwa Indians—Fiction.   2. Indians of North America—Fiction.   3. Babies—Fiction.   4. Dreams—Fiction.
5. Family life—Fiction.]   I. Young, Ed, ill.   II. Title.   PZ7.O8347Dr   1992   [E]—dc20   91-20029

dream
and remember
Ojibway mothers
told their children

in memory
of my son Luther
who shared the
dream

—A.O.

to all those
who respect the gift
and live by the rhythms
of nature

—E.Y.

In the moon of the raspberries
in a time long ago
a baby sleeps,
dreaming.

Dreaming on a cradleboard
wrapped in doeskin soft and snug
a baby sleeps,
smiling.

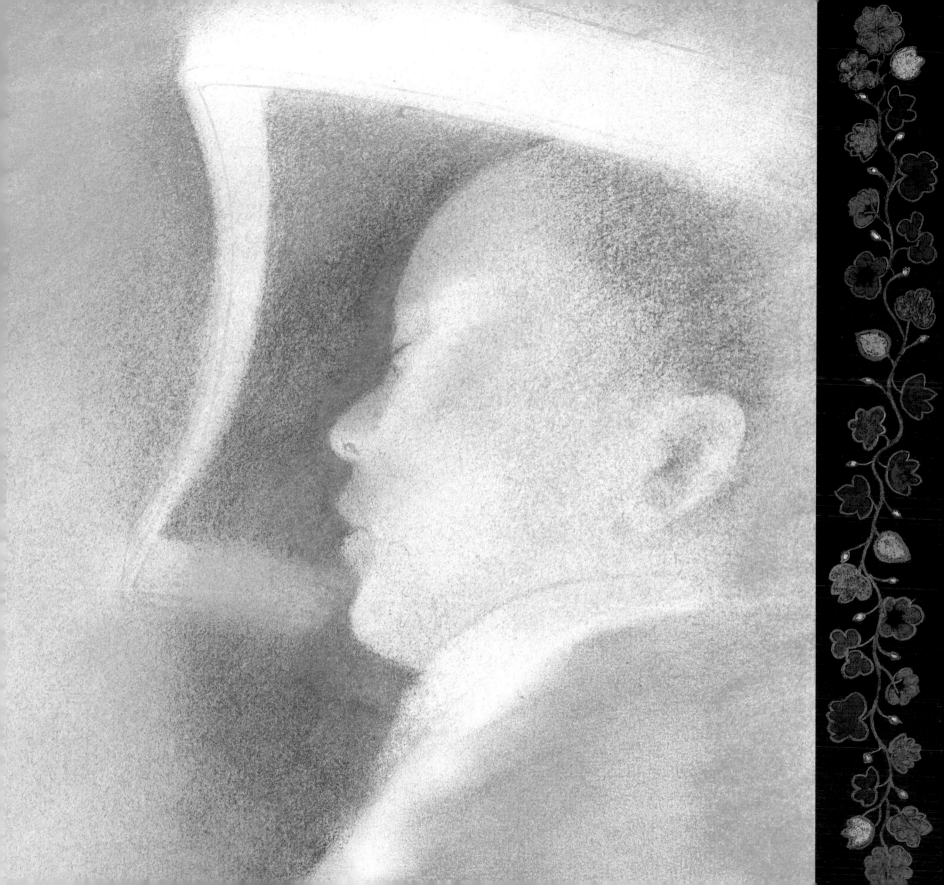

Lullaby, lullaby
sigh the tall pines
as mother picks berries
with baby on her back.

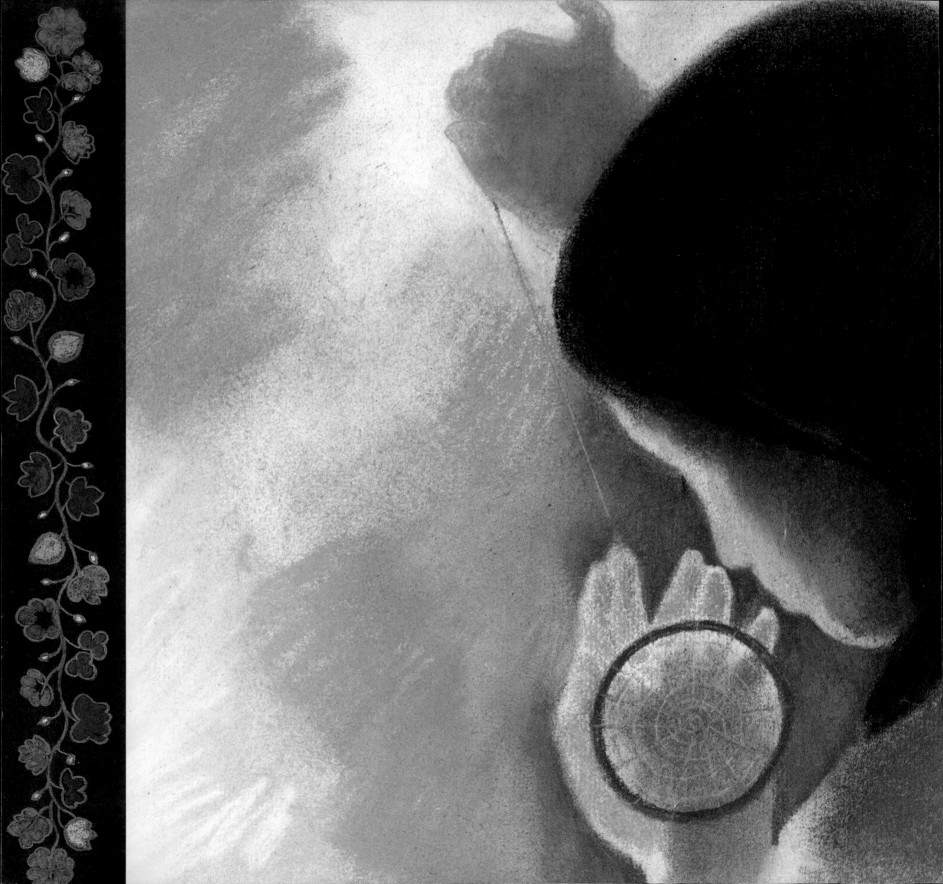

Sleep, baby, sleep
whispers Spirit of the Woods
as big sister weaves a dream net
on a little willow hoop.

A dream net for baby
like a small spiderweb
spun of nettle-stalk twine
stained dark red with the bark of wild plum.

In the land of the Ojibway
in a village by the woods
children play the blindfold game,
calling, "Try to catch me!"

Baby wakes and wonders,
propped under a basswood tree
near mother hoeing the garden,
big sister drying berries in the sun.

Little boys prance by on deer sticks,
kicking up their legs to make baby laugh.

Where shining water meets the shore
mother gathers cattail reeds,
grandmother weaves the mats,
her long deer-bone needle gliding in and out.

"What did you see today that was beautiful?"
she asks big sister weaving her web.
"What did you hear that was pleasing?"
Baby listens, swinging from a low birch limb.

In the blue-sky water
children swim sleek as loons,
dive for clamshells, laugh and splash,
race to meet father skimming in to shore,
fish flopping in his birchbark canoe.
Baby watches, swaying to the swish, swish of waves.

Big sister watches grandmother
stuff a squirrel skin with wild rice,
stitch up the toy for baby,
sees how she knots it tight.
Then sister ties a knot in baby's dream net webbing.

When the sun goes home to sleep,
slipping under a red cloud blanket,
mother wraps baby in rabbit skin,
fluffs dried moss inside the *tikinagan*,
and tucks baby snug for the night.

"Good dreams," wishes big sister
and hangs the net on the cradleboard hoop,
a charm to catch bad dreams.

"Way-ba-ba-way," croons mother,
rocking baby in a hammock
slowly swinging, "way-ba-ba-way"
  sleep baby sleep
  sleep baby sleep
  your dream net will protect you
  sleep baby sleep
  sleep baby sleep
  and dream....

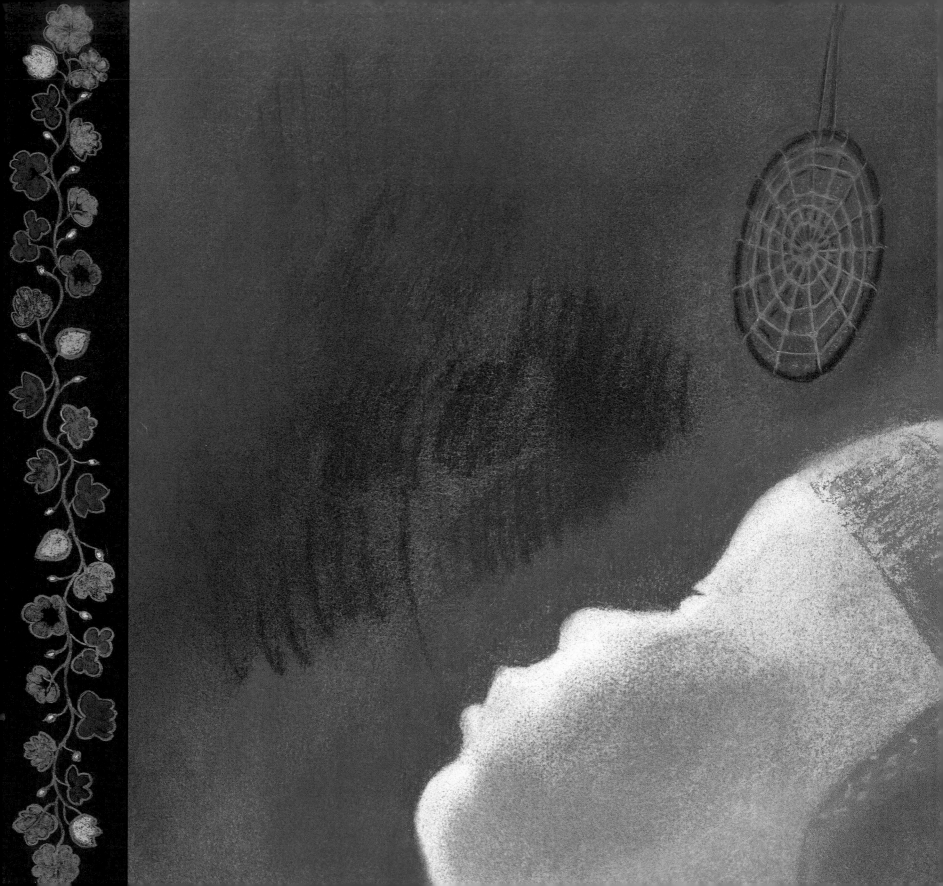

Out of the night swarm dark wings of bad dreams,
but the dream net guards the way.
Tangled in the net, dark dreams are caught
like flies in a spider's web:

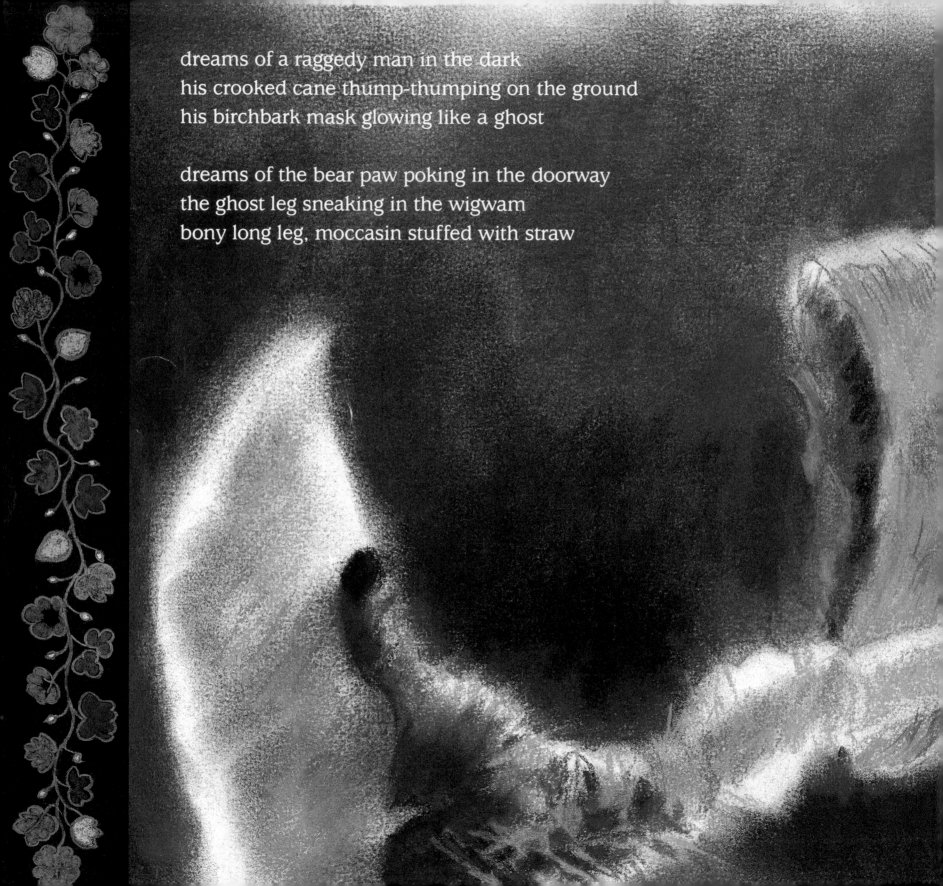

dreams of a raggedy man in the dark
his crooked cane thump-thumping on the ground
his birchbark mask glowing like a ghost

dreams of the bear paw poking in the doorway
the ghost leg sneaking in the wigwam
bony long leg, moccasin stuffed with straw

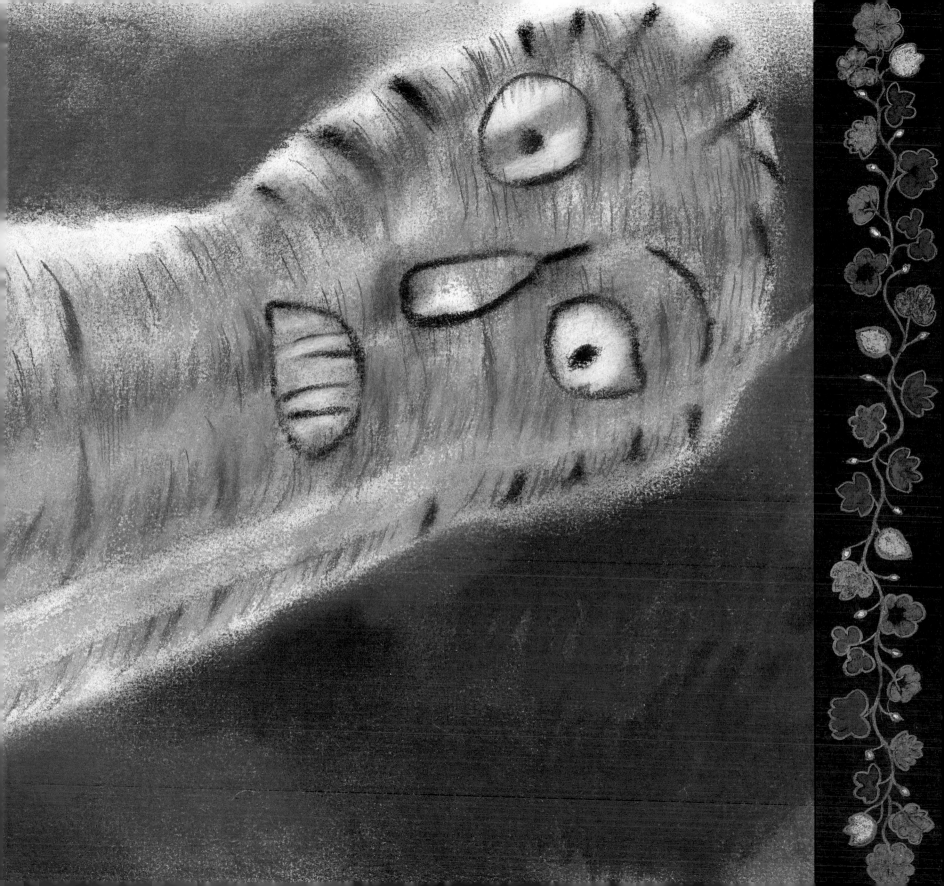

dreams of the owl Kokokoo swooping down from the dark sky
dreams of beating wings, of sharp claws, of feathers flying

caught in the web of the dream net,
while the baby sleeps,
smiling.

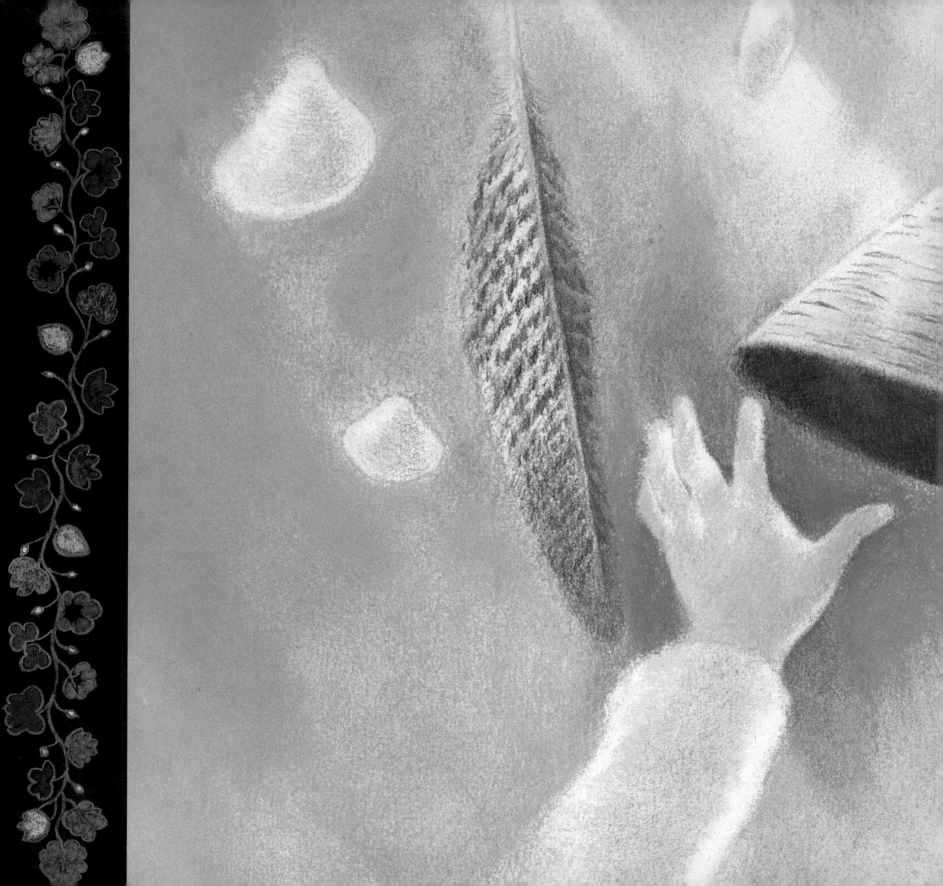

Then softly, like the shadow of a moonbeam,
good dreams drift through the hole in the center of the web:

   dreams of charms hung on the cradleboard—
   little white shells tinkling in the breeze
   pheasant feathers ruffling
   sucking maple sugar in a birchbark cone

dreams of dancing to the beat of the drum
playing leapfrog with the laughing children
racing Brother Squirrel in moccasins fast as flying wings
dreams of chewing on a duck bone

dreams of running in the silk grass of the fields
calling, "Butterfly, butterfly
show me where to go
play hide-and-seek with me."

All night the bad dreams struggle to fight free,
but the dream net holds them fast.
Helpless, the bad dreams die at dawn,
struck by morning light.

In the land of the Ojibway
in a time long ago
a baby sleeps,
dreaming.